To Chloe and Tobi, for joining me on this journey.
—C.K.

For every kid and kid at heart, may you embrace your unique strengths and stay true to yourself!
—C.G.

978-1-953859-31-0 (Hardcover)
978-1-953859-21-1 (Paperback)
978-1-953859-22-8 (E-book)

Library of Congress Control Number: 2021918323

Printed in China

Text by Ceece Kelley
Illustrations by Chloe Guevara
Book design by Tobi Carter
Edited by Nadara "Nay" Merrill

First edition 2022

Soaring Kite Books, LLC
Washington, D.C.
United States of America
www.soaringkitebooks.com

Georgie Dupree
Sharing the Stage

Story by
Ceece Kelley

Pictures by
Chloe Guevara

Soaring Kite Books

"It's even more magical than I dreamed!"

Georgie Dupree's heart flutters at the thought of performing on the big stage for all of her friends and family to see.

She wants to soak up every second and shine on stage. Georgie has to get the part of Alice.

Quinn says,
"I want to be the
Cheshire Cat!
He's so mysterious
and he can
disappear whenever
he wants to."

Camila chimes in,
"I want to be the
Queen of Hearts
and rule the land!"

Maya shouts, "I want to be the
Mad Hatter! Look at me!
I'm so SILLY! I mean MAD!"

Remy points. "I want to help with the special effects and lighting."

Alex says, "I want to be the Caterpillar to help Alice find her way... or not!"

Georgie jumps to the front of the group. "I want to be the lead. I NEED to be Alice!"

Georgie and her friends go home to practice for the big day tomorrow.

She bursts through the house and shouts, "Mama! Daddy!

I have to practice my lines! I need your help, pretty please!"

Georgie pulls Daddy off
of the couch to practice
the scene between Alice
and the Cheshire Cat.

"Shh! No giggles!" Georgie scolds her audience of Mama, Nana, and "The Js"—her twin brothers Julian and James.

Alice: Which way should I go?

Cheshire Cat: Where do you want to end up?

Alice: Well, I don't mind as long as I...

Cheshire Cat: Then you can go whichever way you please!

Daddy hops behind the couch to pretend to disappear like the cat in the story. But he stubs his toe and falls over.

After dinner, Georgie lies in bed and stares at the ceiling as she imagines performing as Alice.

Georgie imagines...

her family cheering loudly from the audience,

her classmates bringing her roses,

and Mr. Parker giving her a high five backstage.

She just has to get the part of Alice.

The next day, Georgie can hardly
wait for her turn on the stage.

"Georgie Dupree, get ready.
You're next!" says Mr. Parker.

"I need to say Alice's lines powerfully
so they can see I'm a perfect fit to
lead the play!" Georgie whispers.

Georgie's voice BOOMS as she reads the lines. She makes big gestures to take up as much of the stage as possible. Alice is the star of the show, after all!

"Well, how did I do?"
Georgie asks with a twirl and a big smile.

"I think everyone in the entire school heard
your audition," Quinn says nervously.

Georgie looks around. *I must have nailed
the audition. Everyone is still watching me!*

Georgie notices that no one else has a powerful audition for Alice like hers.

No one else uses all of the space on the stage like she did.

No one else says their lines as loudly and as clearly as she did.

The part of Alice is mine!

Ananya is the last person to audition for Alice.
She floats across the stage and says her lines sweetly.

Camila leans over to
Georgie and says,
"Wow! She is good!"

Georgie chews her bottom lip.
*I did WOW the audience...
Right?*

Back in class, Georgie waits anxiously for the audition list to be posted.

"Remember, students, no matter who gets which role in the play, we need everyone's help to make the play a success. Break a leg!" cheers Ms. Jaynes.

Finally, the school bell rings and Georgie and her friends run to the theatre buzzing with excitement.

Georgie scans the list, but she does not see her name next to Alice.

It's not next to the White Rabbit.

It's not even next to Tweedle Dee OR Tweedle Dum.

"Congrats, Georgie!" Ananya squeals. "You're Matilda, Alice's big sister! You start and end the show with me, Alice. I'm so excited!"

"Georgie, you're going to be great as Matilda!" says Mr. Parker.

"But I'm only in the play two short times!" Georgie cries.

"Matilda stars in the beginning and end of the play. You also have the opportunity to join the stage teams, background performers, or help run the show's special effects like the lighting."

The cast members celebrate and cheer with excitement.

Everyone except for Georgie Dupree.

Georgie pauses at her doorstep.

Her family knows how much she wanted to be Alice, and now she has to tell them that she didn't get the part.

"Maybe I can sneak up to my room without being seen," Georgie whispers as she opens the door.

3... 2... RUN...!

"There she is! Our Georgie, the star! What part did you get, sugar?" asks Nana.

Drats! Georgie deflates like a balloon.

"I'm not Alice and you'll only get to see me twice. You shouldn't be proud of me," Georgie says quickly as she tries to bolt for the stairs.

"We're always proud of you! When I was in school, we could join the background dancers or help set up the stage too. I'll bet this stage would be fun to design, and you are such a talented artist," adds Mama.

"Don't forget, Georgie. There are many ways to shine," Daddy says with a smile.

Georgie finally makes it to her room after dinner.

"This is my first school play. I wanted to be a star so my family could be proud of me," cries Georgie.

Georgie drifts off to sleep with the play on her mind...

STage TeaM

BackGround PeRFoRMeRS

Matilda: Should I join the background performers or special effects?

Cheshire Cat: Well, that depends on what you enjoy the most.

Matilda: I would get to be on stage more as a background performer...but maybe...I can make the backdrop with the stage team. The backdrops are always on stage!

Cheshire Cat: See...you knew the answer all along. Ta-ta!

SPeCiaL eFFeCTS

"Georgie! Georgie! You're going to be late for your first play rehearsal. Wake up!" warns Nana.

"Wow, Georgie, this is fantastic! This is going to take our play to a whole new level. I'm happy you chose to look on the bright side.

"Thank you, Mr. Parker. I can make a great backdrop for everyone to see. There are many ways to shine!" beams Georgie.

On the night of the play, everyone got a chance to shine on stage, especially Georgie's backdrop.

The End.

Parents & Teachers

THE FUN DOESN'T STOP HERE!

You can find literacy lesson plans for teachers along with a reader's theatre activity at georgiedupree.com.